READ-TOGETHER TREASURY

BEST-LOVED STORIES

publications international, ltd.

A NOTE ABOUT THIS READ-TOGETHER TREASURY

This is a special book. It is designed and written to be shared between an experienced reader and a beginning reader, taking turns reading aloud.

The treasury is extra-wide so that it can be easily spread across two laps. The experienced reader — Mom or Dad, Grandma or Grandpa, even an older brother or sister — sits on the left and reads aloud the left-hand pages. These pages are written using the classic storybook prose that children love to hear, but may not yet be able to read on their own.

The beginning reader sits on the right and reads aloud the right-hand pages. These pages are written especially for early readers. The type is larger and less intimidating, the vocabulary is basic, and the sentences are short and simple.

This book provides the perfect opportunity for a young reader to hone his or her reading and comprehension skills. The positive experience of reading together with a loved one will encourage a love of reading in children. And the quality time spent as you take turns reading may be the greatest reward of all.

Please enjoy this unique book, full of stories to read aloud, stories to treasure…stories to share.

Books are the treasured wealth
of the world and the fit inheritance
of generations and nations.

–Thoreau

TABLE OF CONTENTS

The Three Little Pigs 6

The Princess and the Pea 16

Puss in Boots 26

Goldilocks and the Three Bears 36

The Ugly Duckling 46

The Boy Who Cried Wolf 56

The Four Musicians 66

The Tailor's Apprentices 76

Little Red Riding Hood 86

The Three Little Pigs

Adapted by Shirley Stephenson

Illustrated by Laurie Brackenbury

Early one summer morning, in a

peaceful valley, a mother pig waved goodbye to

her three little pigs as they left for an exciting adventure.

She knew they were going to miss her, but as little pigs grow

older they also grow more independent and curious about the world.

She knew the time had come for them to set out on their own.

The mother loved her little pigs very much, and as they prepared for their journey she reminded them

to make wise choices. "Take care of yourselves," she instructed. "Remember I won't be there to look out for

you. And above all, beware of the big bad wolf, who is known to eat little pigs."

The pigs had a lot of fun. They made new friends. They saw new places.

"Soon it will be cold," said the first pig. "We must find new games."

"Soon it will be cold," said the second pig. "We must save some food."

"Soon it will be cold," said the third pig. "We must build our houses."

The pigs said goodbye and promised to visit each other. Then each pig went off to build a house for himself.

The first little pig followed the road to the right and saw a man carrying a bundle of straw. "Hello, sir," said the pig. "Winter is coming and I need to build my house. May I buy all your straw?"

Happy to make a sale, the man agreed. The little pig chose the closest available land and worked quickly, finishing the house of straw by dinnertime. To celebrate, the little pig ate a big meal, played in the yard, and relaxed beside a nearby stream.

"This is the life!" thought the little pig. "Now I can spend all my days enjoying myself."

And the little pig did just that, until one day when a loud bang shook the walls of the straw house. The little pig looked out the window and saw the big bad wolf standing at the front door. Remembering what his mother had warned him about the wolf, the little pig shivered with fear.

The wolf looked very hungry. "Let me in, little pig, let me in!" yelled the wolf.

"No, no! I will not let you in!" cried the pig. "Not by the hair on my chinny chin chin!"

"Then I'll huff, and I'll puff, and I'll blow your house down!" yelled the wolf.

The little pig would not open the door. The wolf huffed, and he puffed, and, sure enough, he blew the house down. No more house of straw! The little pig ran into the forest and hid from the wolf.

Meanwhile the second little pig had followed the road to the left, searching for the best place to build a home. This little pig decided to build with sticks, and he spent many hours collecting strong pieces of wood. Finally, after several days of work, the house was ready. That night, a cold wind rustled the trees and giant raindrops fell from the sky. The little pig took shelter in the house of sticks.

"This is the life!" thought the second little pig. "Now that I have my own home to keep me warm and dry, I can start a garden so that I will have food to eat and flowers for my yard. Soon, I will invite my two brothers to come visit for a tasty, relaxing meal."

For the next week, the little pig spent each morning planting seeds. When he grew bored with the garden, he played and relaxed. It was a very pleasant life. The only thing the little pig wished for was some company. Then one day a loud knock rattled the walls of the house. The little pig ran to the window, excited to have a visitor. Upon seeing the face at the door, however, the pig's excitement turned to dread.

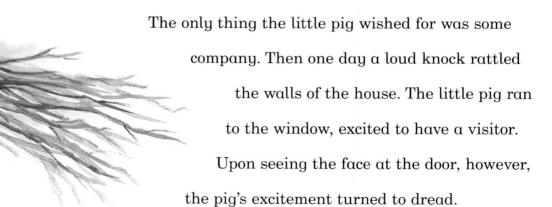

It was the big bad wolf. "Little pig, little pig, let me in!" yelled the wolf.

"Not by the hair on my chinny chin chin!" cried the pig.

"Then I'll huff, and I'll puff, and I'll blow your house down!" yelled the wolf.

The little pig would not open the door. The wolf huffed and he puffed, and, sure enough, he blew the house down. No more house of sticks! The little pig ran into the forest and hid.

The third pig had also built a house, but this little pig used bricks. It was an enormous job. Shortly after the last brick was laid, the big bad wolf pounded on the door. "I'm sorry, Mr. Wolf, but I will not let you in," called the pig. "Not by the hair on my chinny chin chin!"

"Then I'll huff, and I'll puff, and I'll blow your house down!" yelled the wolf. The big bad wolf could not blow down the house. The house had been specially built to keep little pigs safe, warm, and dry. The wolf saved his last breath to call out to the pig. "Little pig, if you meet me tomorrow, I'll bring you to Farmer John's field, where you can help yourself to some tasty turnips."

"Oh, I love turnips," said the pig. They agreed to meet the next day. But that evening, the pig went alone. When the wolf returned, the little pig was back inside, with a cellar full of turnips.

Again the wolf stood outside the brick house. The little pig would not open the door. He was not afraid. The little pig knew he was safe. His house was built of strong bricks.

"Little pig, why did you go without me?" yelled the wolf.
"Because I was hungry," said the pig. "And I like turnips very much."

"Do you also like apples?" asked the wolf.
"Oh, yes! I also like apples," said the pig.

"There is an apple tree near the field," said the wolf. "Meet me there tomorrow at nine o'clock. I am also very hungry so do not be late!"

"No, I will not be late," said the pig.

The next morning, the wolf arrived at the apple tree. Who did he find already resting far out of reach in the highest branches of the tree? That smart little pig! "Good morning," said the little pig. "I picked this bushel of apples for you."

Frustrated, the wolf growled and ran into the forest. The little pig gathered all the ripe apples and returned home. His brothers were waiting for him. Relieved to have found each other, the brothers explained how the wolf blew down their houses of straw and sticks. "Don't worry," said the third little pig. "My brick house will keep us safe, dry, and warm. Plus, I have plenty of food for us to eat. You can stay here through the winter. In the spring we will build two more brick houses together."

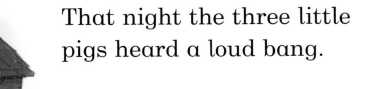

That night the three little pigs heard a loud bang.

"Let me in!" yelled the wolf.

"No," said the pigs. "Not by the hair on our chinny chin chins!"

"Then I will come down the chimney," said the wolf.

"I think it is a bad idea," said the third pig. "You will land in our fire."

The wolf gave up. The three little pigs never saw the big bad wolf again!

The Princess and the Pea

Adapted by Lora Kalkman

Illustrated by Carolyn Croll

There once lived a prince named Philip. More than anything, Prince Philip wanted to marry and have a family of his own.

"Choose your bride carefully," the queen told Prince Philip. "She should be sensitive and kind, thoughtful and wise."

"And above all, she must be a real princess," the king warned.

"How shall I find a special girl like that?" Prince Philip asked.

"We will hold a grand ball," the queen said. "We'll invite princesses from across the land. Surely you will meet a princess who is suitable to marry and whose company you will enjoy."

The day of the ball arrived. Many princesses came.

The girls all wore pretty gowns. Some wore green gowns. Some wore red gowns. Some wore blue gowns. Some wore pink gowns.

Prince Philip greeted each girl. He asked each girl to dance. He spent time with each one.

Some girls were wise. Some were kind. Some were beautiful. Some were funny.

After the ball, Prince Philip was sad. He had not met anyone he wanted to marry.

A few days later, a horse-drawn carriage was traveling near the palace. The grand carriage carried a lovely princess named Rose who was planning to visit her aunt. Princess Rose came from a very distant land. She had not been invited to Prince Philip's ball.

As the carriage approached Prince Philip's palace, the skies grew dark. Before long, droplets of rain splashed down from above. Then it began to storm. The dirt road soon turned to mud.

"Oh no," said the carriage driver. "We are stuck in the mud. What shall we do?"

Princess Rose considered the matter. "There is a castle nearby," she said, pointing to Prince Philip's palace. "I shall inquire about spending the night."

Princess Rose walked to the palace. A light outside led the way.

It rained harder. Her shoes were wet. Her dress was wet.
Her hair was wet, too.

It rained even harder. The ground was very muddy.
Her shoes were muddy. Her dress was muddy, too.

The princess finally reached the castle.
She knocked at the door.

The queen opened the door. The queen was
surprised to see a wet, muddy girl.

"Pardon me, dear lady," said Princess Rose.
"We are stuck in the mud. May we please spend the night?"

The queen did not like the idea. She was about to say no when Prince Philip peered over his mother's shoulder. The prince thought the girl was beautiful, even though her hair and clothes were wet. She had a lovely smile and a pleasant voice.

"Of course you may," Prince Philip said. His mother reluctantly agreed.

The queen sent for towels and fresh clothes. "What is your name?" the queen asked the girl.

"I am Princess Rose," she replied. "I am on my way to visit my aunt."

The queen did not believe the girl was really a princess. After all, the girl was wet and covered with mud! The king agreed with the queen. "No princess would ever let herself get so dirty!" the king said.

Prince Philip, however, believed the girl. He thought she was enchanting.

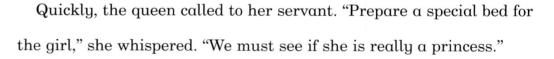

Quickly, the queen called to her servant. "Prepare a special bed for the girl," she whispered. "We must see if she is really a princess." The servant nodded knowingly.

Prince Philip led Princess Rose to her room. She was astonished when she saw the grand bed that had been prepared for her. Princess Rose had never seen such a fancy bed in all her life.

The bed was tall. It had twenty fluffy mattresses. It had twenty fluffy quilts. It had twenty fluffy blankets. The bed had a fluffy pillow, too.

The fluffy mattresses were on the bottom. The fluffy quilts were in the middle. The fluffy blankets were on the top.

The bed was so tall it had a ladder.

"What a fancy bed!" Princess Rose said. "Thank you for your kindness."

"Sweet dreams," said the prince. "I hope you will be comfortable."

Princess Rose put on the lovely nightgown the queen had provided. She was quite tired. After her long day's journey, she looked forward to a cozy night's sleep.

Princess Rose climbed the ladder to the top of the tall, tall bed. The princess admired all of the lovely quilts and blankets. One quilt had pink and yellow stripes. One was yellow with purple polka dots. One was blue with pink triangles. The fluffy blankets had all of the colors of the rainbow. "What a wonderful bed," Princess Rose thought.

Princess Rose rested her head on a pink, fluffy pillow and closed her eyes. Before long, however, she began to toss and turn. The princess was very uncomfortable. She tried and tried, but she just could not sleep.

"There is something lumpy in this bed," the princess said.
"There is something bumpy in this bed," she cried.
"This lumpy, bumpy thing is keeping me awake," she sighed.

Princess Rose was very tired, but she could not sleep. The lumpy, bumpy thing kept her awake all night.

"Could it be a rock?" the princess thought.
"Could it be a bowl?" she said.
"Could it be a ball?" she cried.
"Could it be a lump of coal?" she sighed.

Princess Rose climbed down the ladder.

What was the lumpy, bumpy thing in her tall, cozy bed?

The next morning, Princess Rose met Prince Philip and his parents for breakfast. As she approached, the prince admired her. "I want to marry her," the prince told his parents. "She is sensitive and kind. She is thoughtful and wise."

"First, let's see if she is a princess," the queen replied. "Only a real princess could feel the tiny pea I placed in her bed."

"Good morning," Princess Rose said.

"Good morning," said the king. "Tell me, how did you sleep last night, my dear?"

"Actually, I could not sleep at all," Princess Rose said. "There was something lumpy and bumpy in my bed. I checked to see what it was, and I discovered this tiny, green pea."

The queen was happy. The king was happy. Prince Philip was not surprised at all. Prince Philip knew that Rose was special all along.

The queen had hidden the pea under all the mattresses.
She had hidden the pea under all the quilts. She had hidden the pea under all the blankets. Only a real princess could have felt the pea.

"You are a sensitive girl," said the queen.
"You are a thoughtful girl," said the king.

"And you are very wise, too," said Prince Philip.
"Princess Rose, will you marry me?"

"I will," said Princess Rose.

A wedding was held. And they all lived happily every after.

Puss In Boots

Adapted by Sharon Cronk-Raby

Illustrated by Julius and Victoria Lisi

Puss was a smart cat. When his master, a farmer, was too old to care for him, Puss went to talk to the farmer's son.

"I am looking for a new home," Puss told the son. "I have been very loyal to your father. Now, I want to be loyal to you."

The son did not know if he wanted a cat. He did not have very much money, and he didn't know if he could take care of Puss as well as his father had. The son told Puss that he would have to earn his keep.

Puss gladly agreed.

"I will work very hard for you," Puss said. "I am a smart cat, and a good hunter, too."

"I could use a strong hunter," the son said.

"May I have a pair of boots, please?" Puss asked.

"Boots?" asked the son. He had never heard of a cat wearing boots.

"Oh yes," said Puss. "Hunters need boots."

"Very well," said the son.

The next day, Puss had a new pair of boots. He was very happy. He had a plan.

Puss would make his new master very proud. Puss knew the king liked rabbits and partridges. He also knew no one else was having any luck capturing such treasures for the king's feasts, not even the greatest hunters. Puss was a good hunter, and he had caught many mice on the farm. He knew that he would easily be able to catch rabbits and partridges for the king, especially in his boots.

Puss set out into the woods. He was able to catch many rabbits and many partridges that he placed into his sack and carried to the king. When Puss presented these items as gifts to the king, instead of saying they were from the son of a farmer, he said they were presents from a duke, the Duke of Carabas. The king was delighted! At first, people could not believe that a cat, wearing boots, was allowed in the palace. But then they heard about the wonderful gifts the cat presented to the king on behalf of the duke. Everyone began to talk about the Duke of Carabas. Everyone was curious to learn more about him.

Each day, Puss brought gifts to the king.
Each day, the king was more and more happy.

"What lovely rabbits!" the king said.
"What beautiful birds!" he cheered.
"What perfect presents!" he shouted.

"I am glad you like them," Puss said.

"The duke is a fantastic hunter," the king said.
"I would like to meet him."

"He is a very smart man," Puss said.

The king called to his men.
"Tomorrow we will visit the duke," he said.

The next day the king, the king's men, and the king's daughter rode their carriage out to the country to find the duke. Everyone was anxious to meet him.

Puss knew they would be driving past the river. Puss asked the farmer's son to come with him. The son followed Puss to the river. Then Puss asked him to jump into the river. When he refused, Puss gently pushed him into the water.

"I'll explain later, sir," Puss whispered.

As the carriage approached, Puss shouted, "Help! The Duke of Carabas is drowning! Thieves robbed him and pushed him in the river!"

The king's men stopped and came to the rescue. The king instantly recognized the puss in boots.

The farmer's son felt like a fool. He thought his cat was smart, but he had gotten him into trouble with the king! However, the king was happy to help the duke who had provided him with so many wonderful gifts.

"The duke is very wet!" the king said to his men. "Please go get new clothes for him."

The king turned to the duke, "Will you sit with my daughter and me in the carriage?"

The princess was very happy! She liked the duke very much.

The farmer's son was confused. He did not know why people thought he was a duke.

Puss smiled. He was a very smart cat.

The king's men returned with beautiful new clothes for the duke.

While the king was busy with the son, a man he thought to be a duke, Puss, who was a very smart cat, continued on with his plan. Puss ran ahead of the carriage, where he found some farmhands in a field.

"Do you want the king to be pleased with you?" Puss asked the men.

"Yes!" they answered at once.

"Good," said Puss. "When the king asks you who owns these fields, you must tell him the Duke of Carabas does. That will make everyone happy!"

The farmhands wanted to make the king happy, so they agreed.

Puss continued down the road. He gave these same instructions to everyone he met. Puss wanted the king to think his master was very rich and successful. This was all part of his plan.

The king's carriage came to the field. Puss hid behind the corn. The farmhands stopped working to wave to their king.

"Hello!" said the king. "Who owns this wonderful land?"

The people wanted to make the king happy. "The duke owns this land," they said.

The king's carriage came to the next field. Again, the people waved.

"Hello!" the king said. "Who owns this wonderful land?"

"The Duke of Carabas owns this land," the people said.

Puss, who was a very smart cat, ran ahead to a large castle that belonged to a big, mean giant. It was the giant who really owned the land. Puss bravely knocked on the door of the castle.

"Who are you?" roared the big, mean giant. "I have never seen a cat with boots!"

"Sir," Puss said. "I have heard of your great talents. I would like to see some of your tricks."

The giant was very grumpy, but he was also very proud of his tricks. "I know many tricks," the giant said.

"Can you turn yourself into a lion?" Puss asked. "I'd like to see it."

The giant turned himself into a big, angry lion.

Puss pretended to be very frightened. "What a wonderful trick," said Puss. "I liked that trick, but can you turn yourself into a small animal, too?"

The giant smiled. These were not difficult tricks for a giant. He closed his eyes, took a deep breath, and turned himself into a tiny mouse.

Puss, who was a very smart cat, quickly ate him! The farmer's son would now have all the possessions of a very rich man.

The king's carriage came to the castle. "Who owns this big castle?" asked the king.

"My master, the duke!" Puss said. "Won't you all come in for a feast?"

"You are very rich," the king said.
"I am?" said the farmer's son.
"You are!" said Puss.

"How did you get so rich?" asked the king.

"I have a very smart friend," said the duke.

Goldilocks and the Three Bears

Adapted by Rebecca Grazulis

Illustrated by David Merrell

Once there was a family of three bears. Baby Bear was a small, wee bear. Mama Bear was a middle-sized bear, and Papa Bear was a great, huge bear. Every morning the bears made porridge for breakfast. One morning the porridge was especially hot. "My little tongue will be burned!" said Baby Bear. The bears went for a walk while their porridge cooled.

The bears didn't know that a girl named Goldilocks had spotted the steaming bowls through the window.

Goldilocks was very hungry.
"This looks tasty!" she said.
"I will just take a little bite."

Goldilocks tasted the porridge
from Papa Bear's bowl.
"Oh no, this porridge
is too hot!" she said.

Goldilocks tasted the porridge from Mama Bear's bowl. "Oh no, this porridge is too cold!" she said.

Goldilocks tasted the porridge from Baby Bear's wee bowl. "This porridge is just right!" she said.

Goldilocks ate all of Baby Bear's porridge. She did not leave a single bite.

Goldilocks patted her full stomach happily. All that porridge made her tired. Goldilocks began exploring the bear's home. She came upon their living room, which held three chairs. Goldilocks decided to try each of the chairs. First she sat in the biggest chair, which was Papa Bear's. It was tall and wooden and very sturdy. "This chair is too hard," Goldilocks frowned.

Goldilocks decided to try Mama Bear's chair. Mama Bear's chair was a bit smaller and a very pretty blue color. But Goldilocks didn't appreciate Mama Bear's chair either. "This chair is too soft!" she said.

Baby Bear's chair was the last chair Goldilocks tried. When Goldilocks sat down in Baby Bear's chair a smile spread across her face. "This chair is just right!" she said happily.

But Goldilocks liked the chair a little too much. She sat back and rocked in the chair, swinging her legs back and forth. Perhaps she was a little too big for Baby Bear's wee chair because, with a crack and a loud thud, the chair broke into pieces under her weight. Goldilocks fell to the ground.

Goldilocks looked around the house for a place to rest. She found a cozy room with three beds. Goldilocks yawned. Her eyelids drooped. She was getting sleepy.

Goldilocks lay down on Papa Bear's bed. "This bed is too hard," she said.

Goldilocks tried Mama Bear's bed. "This bed is too soft," she said.

Goldilocks lay down on Baby Bear's bed. It was a small, wee bed. "This is just right," Goldilocks said.

Goldilocks pulled the covers up to her chin and closed her eyes. She fell asleep. She even snored!

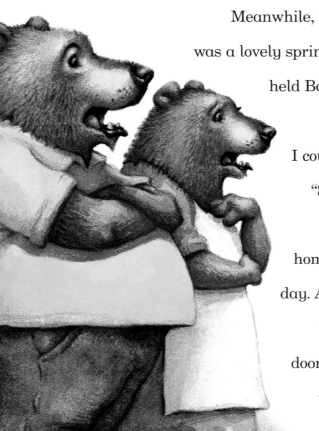

Meanwhile, the bear family was strolling happily through the woods. It was a lovely spring day and they were enjoying the fresh air. Mama Bear held Baby Bear's paw in hers. Papa Bear whistled as he walked.

"Isn't it a great day, Papa?" exclaimed Baby Bear. "I wish I could stay outside all day."

"Sounds good to me!" agreed Papa Bear.

"Let's not forget that we have breakfast waiting for us at home," said Mama Bear. "It is the most important meal of the day. After breakfast we can come back outside and play."

The bears walked back home. When they reached the front door, they noticed that it was slightly ajar. Slowly, the bears walked inside. Something was just not right. Somebody had been in their home.

"Who would do such a thing?" asked Mama Bear.

"I don't know," said Papa Bear with a frown.

The bears went into their kitchen. Something was not right.
There was a spoon in Papa Bear's bowl.
Papa Bear saw it. He was very surprised.
"Somebody has been eating my porridge!" Papa Bear said.

There was a spoon in Mama Bear's bowl, too.
"Somebody has been eating my porridge!" she said.

Baby Bear was holding his small, wee bowl.
The bowl was empty. All the porridge was gone!
"Somebody has been eating my porridge," Baby
Bear said. "And that somebody has eaten it all up!"

Baby Bear started to cry. He was hungry.

"Who would do such a thing?" asked Mama Bear.

Now, the bears were good bears and never did anybody any harm. They were very kind to their neighbors and were always helping out around the forest. So they never suspected that anyone would break in to their house, much less eat their porridge!

Mama Bear was very upset. She wrung her hands and paced the room. "I don't understand!" she cried. "I would make porridge for anyone. Why didn't they just ask?"

Baby Bear stared into his empty bowl and wiped the tears from his fur. "Not a drop left," he said sadly. "And I'm so hungry!"

"Let's go sit down and sort this out," Papa Bear suggested.

Mama Bear took Baby Bear by the hand and led him into the living room. Papa Bear followed close behind. When they reached the living room, Baby Bear started to cry again.

"Baby Bear," said Mama Bear, "what's wrong?"

"My chair!" Baby Bear cried. "My chair has been broken to pieces!"

"Who would do such a thing?" asked Mama Bear.

Papa Bear walked over to his chair.
The cushion was not straight.
"Somebody has been sitting in my chair,"
Papa Bear said.

Mama Bear walked over to her chair.
The cushions were all smushed.
"Somebody has been sitting in my chair,"
Mama Bear said.

The bear family was sad.
Baby Bear was the saddest.
His little chair was the perfect size.

"Who would do such a thing?"
Mama Bear asked.

Papa Bear was trying to be brave, but he was feeling pretty low. Mama Bear was frightened. Baby Bear was crying. What was a Papa Bear to do? Finally Papa Bear summoned up his courage. He marched into the center of the living room and put his hands on his hips. He had an idea. "I know what we need to do," Papa Bear said. "We are going to go take a nap. Bears always feels better after a nap."

The three Bears shuffled to their bedroom.

Soon the Bears saw that things were not in order. In fact, everything was a mess! Goldilocks had rearranged the pillows on Papa Bear's bed. "Somebody has been lying in my bed!" roared Papa Bear.

Mama Bear noticed that her blanket was rumpled. "Somebody has been lying in my bed!" she cried.

Then Baby Bear looked at his bed. He rubbed his eyes. "Somebody has been sleeping in my bed," Baby Bear said, "and that somebody is still sleeping!"

"Wake up, little girl," Papa Bear said.

"Who is she?" asked Mama Bear.

"Ask her why she ate my breakfast,"
Baby Bear said with his wee voice.

Baby Bear's voice woke Goldilocks.
Goldilocks was afraid. She jumped
up and climbed out the open window.
She ran all the way home. The
bears never saw her again.

Goldilocks learned her lesson.
No matter how hungry she was,
she would never eat a bear's breakfast again.

The Ugly Duckling

Adapted by Elizabeth Olson

Illustrated by John Manders

One fine spring day, a mother duck sat on her nest at the edge of a pond.

Although the day was bright and fresh, the mother duck was tired. She had

spent most of the spring sitting on her eggs. Finally they began to crack.

One by one, three little yellow ducklings tumbled out of their shells.

"Peep! Peep! Peep!" they called to the world.

"Quack! Quack! Quack!" answered the mother duck.

The mother admired her new family. But what was this?

The largest egg had not yet hatched. With a sigh, the

mother duck sat back

down on her last egg.

The mother duck waited. And she waited. And she waited. Finally, the egg cracked. A big, gray, baby bird popped out of the shell.

"Peep! Peep! Peep!" said the baby bird.

"Quack! Quack! Quack!" said the mother duck. She was very surprised. This duck did not look like its brothers or sisters.

The baby waddled through the grass. He was clumsy. His legs looked too small for his body.

"You sure are an odd duckling," said the mother. "Still I love you just the same as the others."

The next day, the mother duck took her little ones to the pond. The ducklings jumped into the water one at a time. They paddled their feet and swam. Even the big, gray duckling swam. "See how well he uses his legs and holds his head," said the mother duck. "In a way, he is handsome."

The proud mother duck took all her ducklings to the farmyard. "Follow me," she told them. "Stay in line and say, "Quack!" All the ducklings obeyed, including the big, gray duckling.

In the farmyard, the other ducks pointed at the big, gray duckling and called him names. "Look at the ugly duckling!" they laughed.

"Leave him alone," said the mother duck. "He may be a bit large, and gray, too, but he is handsome in his own way."

But the farmyard ducks did not leave the gray duckling alone. "Ugly ducking! Ugly duckling! Look at the ugly duckling!" they sang.

The big, gray duckling hung his head. He was very sad.

"Come along, children," said the mother duck. The ducklings lined up behind their mother.

"Quack! Quack!" said the yellow ducklings. The gray duckling was quiet.

The mother duck and her ducklings waddled back to the pond. The big, gray duckling walked behind the others. "No one likes me," he said. "I am just an ugly duckling."

The mother duck stopped at the pond's edge. "Quack! Quack! Quack!" she called.

The yellow ducklings jumped into the water. The mother duck stopped the ugly duckling. "Don't let the farmyard ducks bother you," she said. "You are beautiful in your own way. Someday everyone will see that."

"Do you really think so?" said the ugly duckling, raising his lowered head.

"Yes I do. Now join the others," she said, encouraging him with a quick "Quack!"

The ugly duckling jumped into the water. His mother's words made him feel warm inside. Maybe he wouldn't always be an ugly duckling! He paddled his strong legs. He was a good swimmer and soon passed all the other ducklings. Before realizing what he had done, the ugly duckling had crossed the pond. On the other side, he looked around for his mother and the others but did not see them.

The little duckling swam and swam. He could not find his mother.

"Woof! Woof! Woof!" barked a dog.
"Buzz! Buzz! Buzz!" A dragonfly flew from the grasses.
"Woof! Woof! Woof!" barked the dog again.

The dog snapped at the dragonfly. The dragonfly flew up high and landed on a leaf. The curious dog sniffed it.

Two feet away, the ugly duckling hid in the tall grasses. He stood very still. He was afraid.

Then, with a shake of its tail, the dog ran away. The ugly duckling was alone.

The ugly duckling stayed near the pond all summer. Every day he swam in the water and waited for his mother. Soon the air became cooler and the leaves turned yellow and brown. The ugly duckling saw a flock of elegant, white birds fly overhead. The ugly duckling wished he could follow them. He was too small.

When the water started to freeze and the air was cold, the ugly duckling left the pond. He waddled until he saw a cozy farmhouse.

The ugly duckling jumped onto the window ledge and peered inside. He saw a warm fire and a tiny pond of water. The ugly duckling walked into the warm house and jumped into the little pond. The water felt so good. He decided he would wait for his mother there.

The farmer's wife heard a splish! The farmer's wife heard a splash! Splish! Splash! The farmer's wife heard something in the bathtub!

"What on earth?" she asked. "Why is there a duck in the bathtub?"

The farmer's wife scared the ugly duckling. He flapped his wings. Water flew up in the air. Slish! Water spilled on the floor. Slosh! Slish! Slosh! There was water everywhere!

The farmer's wife shouted and grabbed her broom. Swoosh! She chased the ugly duckling out the door.

The sad ugly duckling was alone again.

Outside the air was cold. The ugly duckling wrapped his little wings around himself and slept. In his dreams he swam across blue waters and felt the golden sunshine.

Finally, spring had arrived. The ugly duckling lifted his neck and stretched his wings. He walked to the pond. In the water he saw an elegant, white bird. "I am sorry to bother you," said the ugly duckling, "but may I swim here with you?"

"Silly swan," answered a frog. "You are talking to your own reflection."

"I'm not a swan," the ugly duckling said.

"And I thought only the goose was silly," the frog said with a laugh. "Look again. Everyone, even you, can see that you, my friend, are a beautiful swan."

The ugly duckling looked again. The frog was right. He had beautiful, white feathers. He had a beautiful, graceful neck. He had beautiful, long wings. He was not an ugly duckling.

Two more swans swam toward him. "Are you lost?" they asked.

"I am waiting for my mother," he said.

"Come wait with us. We can swim together," they said.

The beautiful swan smiled. He was proud. He was happy. He made his first new friends.

The Boy Who Cried Wolf

Adapted by Lora Kalkman

Illustrated by Jon Goodell

In a faraway land of green pastures and bright skies, there lived a little boy. The boy's name was Thomas. He was nine years old.

Thomas lived with his family in a village nestled in the foothills of a grand mountain. It was a lovely little village. Many of the people who lived in town were farmers. Some of them raised sheep. The sheep liked to roam and graze in the green pasture.

All of the village children had chores to do. Thomas' job was to watch over the sheep.

Each morning, Thomas led the sheep to pasture.

"Come, come!" he shouted to the big mother ewes.

"Come, come!" he shouted to the big father rams and the little baby lambs.

One by one, the sheep followed Thomas to the pasture.

Thomas spent his days alone with the sheep. He brought a ball to the pasture. Sometimes he would invent games to play by himself. He would kick the ball across the grass while chanting, "Kick the ball, then run and leap, but never touch a single sheep!"

Other times, he would pass the time counting. "One, two, three, the sheep will follow me."

Thomas could also count by twos. "Two, four, six, I'll teach my sheep some tricks."

He could even count by threes. "Three, six, nine, I'll bring them back on time."

Thomas enjoyed watching the sheep, but he missed playing with people. Sometimes, when Thomas grew tired of his games, he would gaze off toward the village. "I wonder if anyone ever thinks about me out here," he thought.

One day, Thomas felt lonely.
He looked out at the sheep.
He looked out at the faraway village.

"I wish I had someone to play with," he said.

He was tired of playing ball. He was tired of counting sheep. Tending sheep was not very exciting.

Thomas thought about the dark forest nearby. "I'll bet the forest is exciting," he thought.

Thinking about the forest made Thomas remember what his parents said about wolves. Wolves like to eat sheep, which is why Thomas had to watch out for them. Thomas had never seen a wolf. Thomas wondered what would happen if a wolf were to come to the pasture. A wolf would add some excitement.

"If there was a wolf," Thomas thought proudly, "it would be my important job to call for help. Everyone would come running. I would save the sheep. I would be a hero!"

Thomas grew more and more excited about being a hero. He wished that a wolf would come. But no matter how hard Thomas wished, a wolf never emerged from the deep, dark forest.

Finally, Thomas grew tired of waiting. "I could just pretend there is a wolf," he thought.

Thomas thought it was an excellent idea. He began to shout, "Help! Help! Wolf! Wolf! There's a wolf in the pasture, and he sure looks hungry!"

The people in town heard Thomas' cry.
They ran to the pasture. They ran to save
Thomas and the sheep.

Thomas smiled. His trick had worked.

The villagers did not see a wolf.
They only found a smiling boy.

"Are you sure you saw a wolf,
Thomas?" the villagers asked.

Thomas tried not to laugh.

"I guess there was no wolf after
all," Thomas said with a giggle.

The villagers searched the pasture, just in case. They searched behind trees. They searched behind bushes.

When they didn't find a wolf, they were very relieved. Finally, all of the villagers returned to town.

Thomas smiled happily. He enjoyed the excitement.

The next day, Thomas led his sheep to the pasture. As usual, he played with his ball. Then he watched the clouds.

Then he counted his sheep by ones, then by twos, then by threes. Again the little boy grew bored.

"It was more fun when the villagers came," Thomas thought.

Thomas looked out toward the deep, dark forest, took a big breath, and began to shout out toward the village, "Help! Help! Wolf! Wolf! There's a wolf in the pasture, and he sure looks hungry!"

The people in town heard Thomas' cry. They ran to the pasture. They ran to save Thomas and the sheep.

Thomas laughed. His trick had worked again. "There is no wolf," Thomas said.

This made the villagers angry.

"You must not lie," a farmer said. "You must always tell the truth or people will never believe you."

Thomas was sorry. He learned his lesson. He promised not to lie again.

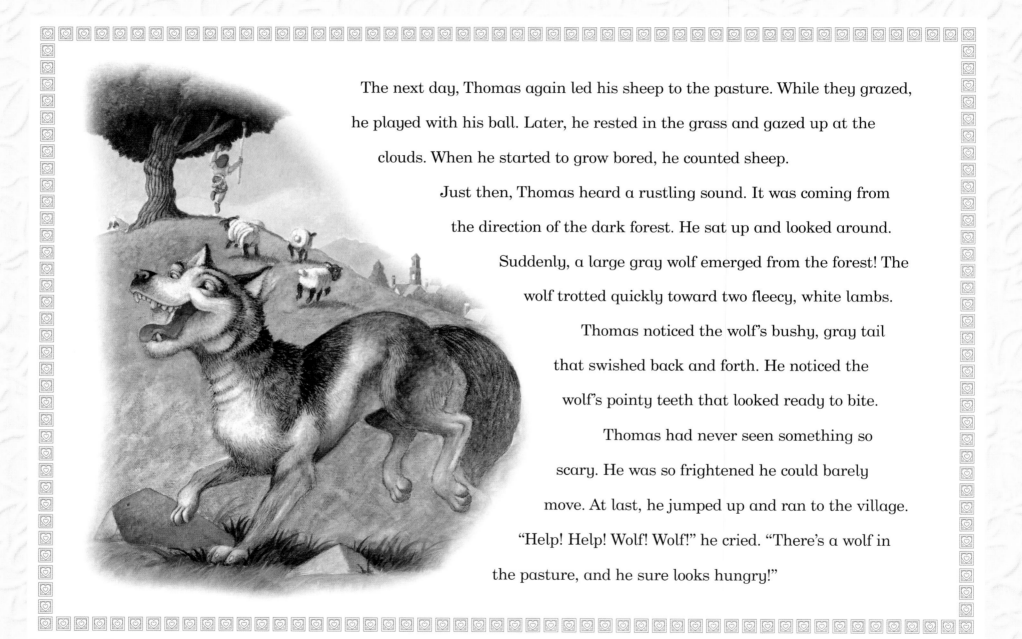

The next day, Thomas again led his sheep to the pasture. While they grazed, he played with his ball. Later, he rested in the grass and gazed up at the clouds. When he started to grow bored, he counted sheep.

Just then, Thomas heard a rustling sound. It was coming from the direction of the dark forest. He sat up and looked around.

Suddenly, a large gray wolf emerged from the forest! The wolf trotted quickly toward two fleecy, white lambs.

Thomas noticed the wolf's bushy, gray tail that swished back and forth. He noticed the wolf's pointy teeth that looked ready to bite.

Thomas had never seen something so scary. He was so frightened he could barely move. At last, he jumped up and ran to the village.

"Help! Help! Wolf! Wolf!" he cried. "There's a wolf in the pasture, and he sure looks hungry!"

This time the villagers did not run to help. They did not believe him.

The wolf stole the sheep.

The villagers were glad that Thomas was not hurt. But they were upset about losing their sheep.

Thomas felt sad, too. He wanted excitement, but he did not want to lose his sheep.

"A liar will not be believed, even when he tells the truth," one farmer reminded him.

Thomas learned his lesson—the hard way.

The Four Musicians

Adapted by Lynne Roberts
Illustrated by Wendy Edelson

Once there was a donkey who worked hard in the fields every day. He pulled the farmer's cart to and from the market. He gave the farmer's children rides to the sweet shop. But now his tired back ached with every load.

The farmer knew the donkey was getting old. His neighbor suggested that he buy a tractor to work his fields, or a shiny new truck to haul his heavy loads.

The donkey heard the two men speak. He felt useless. "I'm going to run away," said the donkey. "I'll go to the town of Bremen and become a musician." The donkey left for town the next day.

On the road the donkey met a sad dog. "I'm useless," said the dog.

"That cannot be true," said the donkey. "Come to Bremen. We can be singers."

The old dog was happy. "I do have a nice howl," he said.

On the road they met an old cat. The cat was crying.

"Why the long whiskers?" the dog asked.

The old cat cried and said, "My owner thinks I'm too old to catch mice. I am useless."

The donkey and the dog smiled at the old cat. "You should come with us," said the dog. "Do you sing?"

"We are going to town to become musicians!" the donkey said.

"I do have a nice purr!" said the cat. The old cat jumped off the fence and joined them on their journey.

The three new friends began to sing, but soon they were interrupted by a strange crowing sound.

The crowing came from an old rooster.

"Cock-a-doodle-doo! I don't know what to do!" cried the rooster. "I'm too old to get up at the crack of dawn. My owner wants to cook me for Sunday dinner," he said.

"Do you sing?" the donkey, the dog, and the cat asked all at once. They invited the rooster to join them on their trip.

"Don't worry," said the cat with a warm smile. "We will only sing at night."

"Thank you, friends," said the rooster. "I do have a strong crow."

The friends walked and walked. They could not make it to Bremen that day. The sky turned dark.

The four friends wanted to find a house to sleep in. They settled for a nice tree.

The cat climbed into the branches. The rooster flew up to the top. The donkey and dog rested in the soft grass.

"Wait!" said the rooster. "There is a light over there. I see a house."

The dog, the cat, the donkey, and the rooster left the tree. They walked in the direction of the house.

"I wonder who lives in this house," said the donkey.

"I hope they have something to eat," said the dog.

"I hope they have something to eat and a nice warm fire to curl up next to," said the cat.

The friends looked at the glowing light from the window. It was too high for them to see inside.

"What should we do?" asked the rooster, jumping up and down and flapping his wings.

The donkey had a plan. He told the dog to climb on his back. Then the cat was to climb on the dog's back. Then the rooster was to fly up on top of the cat's back. Together they would be tall enough to see inside the window.

Up climbed the dog. Up climbed the cat.
Up flew the rooster.

"We can see," said the rooster.
"I cannot believe my eyes," said the dog.

They saw a table full of food and money.
The friends were excited.

"We should sing," said the rooster.
"We can sing for food," said the dog.

The donkey sang with his loud,
booming voice. The dog howled. The
cat sang. The rooster crowed. They
sang as loudly as they knew how.

What the four did not know was that the people inside the cozy house were thieves! The thieves were counting their money when they heard the noise coming from outside their window. The noise did not sound like singing to the thieves' ears. To them, the noise sounded like a monster howling and crying in the darkness.

"Do you hear that noise?" asked one thief.

"It must be evil spirits, punishing us because we took this money!" said another thief.

The thieves were scared at the idea of evil spirits haunting them for taking the money. Quickly, they all ran from the house. They did not see the donkey, the dog, the cat, and the rooster standing at the window.

The thieves ran until they were deep in the woods.

The friends went inside the house.

The cat smiled as he sat at the table. The dog licked his lips and sat by the cat. The rooster perched on a chair with a flap of his feathers.

The donkey cut a piece of pie for each of them.

"What a yummy meal," said the rooster.

"My tummy is nice and full," said the cat.

The thieves stayed in the woods for hours. They did not know if the monster was still lurking outside their house. Finally, one thief said, "I have had enough! I am cold and I am tired. Monster or no monster, I'm going home."

In the dark house the thief saw two glowing eyes by the fireplace! He did not know that he was looking at the cat, who was curled up by the hearth. The thief screamed. The cat was startled and scratched his face. The thief tried to get out the door, but he stepped on the dog's tail. The dog bit the thief's leg.

In all the commotion, the donkey kicked the thief in the head. The thief was dizzy and confused. When the rooster began to crow from the rafters, the thief thought the noise was the evil spirits coming after him. He made his way out of the house and never came back.

The four friends were shocked.
The thief made a big mess!

The next morning the
friends ate a nice big meal.
Then they walked to town.

"The townspeople will love
our music," said the dog.

"Yes," said the donkey.
"Look at what a smash
we were last night!"

The four singers laughed
and began their song.

The Tailor's Apprentices

Adapted by Leslie Lindecker

Illustrated by Mike Jaroszko

There once was a poor tailor who talked to the mice who lived beneath the floor as he sewed. "Someday, my friends," the tailor said, "my work will be rewarded. Until then you must appreciate the snips that are too small for me to use." Someday came sooner than the tailor had expected, for just then the town's mayor visited the tailor's shop. The mayor was getting married and needed the tailor to make his suit. "With great pride I will make you a fine suit," the tailor said.

The tailor laughed. He danced around his shop. He called to the mice.
"My little friends," the tailor said, "I am a lucky man.
I am going to make the mayor's suit for his wedding day!
I will find perfect pieces of green satin.
I will find the most beautiful golden thread.
I will find the finest lace in all the land!"

The mice giggled. If the tailor was
lucky, they would be lucky, too!

The mice would have the best
scraps of satin, the best
bits of golden thread,
and the finest
snips of lace in
all the world!

The tailor measured and marked, and measured again. He cut out the coat from the emerald cloth.

"No waste on this fabric. Such a grand suit this will be, all stitched with gold!" the tailor said.

Soon the table was covered with pieces of coat and parts of vest. Everything was ready to begin sewing the emerald suit except for one spool of golden thread. The tailor took off his glasses and rubbed his eyes.

"We will begin in the morning, my friends," the tailor said. "It is too dark to sew tonight."

The tailor walked out of his shop into the December night. He locked the door and put the key into his pocket. He shuffled up the rickety stairs to the room he rented above his shop.

The tailor lived alone with his cat. As he unlocked the door, the cat meowed and rubbed against his feet. "Tomkin, old friend," the tailor said, "good luck is with us, but I am terribly tired tonight. I may have a touch of the flu."

The tailor took a scrap of paper and made a list.

"Tomkin," the tailor said, "Please go to the store. We need a few things. We need a bottle of milk. We need a bit of bread. And I need a spool of golden thread for the mayor's new wedding suit."

The tailor tied the list and his last dollar to Tomkin's collar. The old tailor crawled into his bed to get warm.

Tomkin walked out into the cold night. He did not like the cold, but he did like a cup of milk to help wash down his supper.

The tailor woke up to a *tip-tip-tap*. He looked around and saw his teacups and bowls turned upside down. He heard the *tip-tip-tap* again. The tailor got up, lifted a teacup, and out popped a lovely lady mouse. He looked under a bowl and found a handsome gentleman mouse.

"I truly must be ill, for that mouse I saw was wearing a hat!" said the tailor. The tailor turned over the teacups and bowls to find many little mice hopping and bobbing and running about in their finest clothes.

The tailor talked to himself as he went back to bed. The little mice listened to the tailor as he muttered about the suit for the mayor. The mice squeaked and scampered away.

Just then Tomkin nudged open the door. He was not happy. He was cold and hungry. He jumped up on the table and dropped the sack he carried in his mouth containing the bottle of milk, the bit of bread, and the spool of thread.

Tomkin spied the overturned teacups and upturned bowls. With a snarl, he swatted a cup to the floor in search of the fat little mice.

"Tomkin, is that you?" the tailor asked from his bed. "I hope you remembered to get my spool of golden thread."

"What did you do with my mice?" Tomkin asked. "I worked all day to catch those mice. They were going to be my supper!"

Tomkin hunted through the room. He looked behind doors. He checked inside cabinets. He peeked under the bed. He listened for tiny footsteps. He listened for squeaks. Tomkin could not find a single mouse for supper. Tomkin was so angry, he hid the spool of thread under a teapot.

The tailor stayed in bed for several days, too sick to work. He had a terrible fever. He mumbled about the mayor's new suit and cried out with the need for a spool of golden thread. Tomkin meowed for the little mice that were lost, and he fed on the bit of bread and the bottle of milk he had fetched a few days before.

It was the day before the mayor's wedding, and the town was beginning to celebrate. Tomkin went outside to find out what was going on. That is when he heard voices coming from inside the tailor's small shop.

Tomkin leapt upon the window ledge and peeked into the shop. In the candlelight, Tomkin could see his little mice, the same ones the tailor had let go, singing and dancing — and sewing! They were stitching the emerald coat with golden thread. They sang as they sewed lace to the vest. They danced about in mouse hats and mouse vests they had made from the scraps and ribbons and threads the tailor had left for them.

The little mice sang to make the time go faster.

See the little mice sitting down to sew.
Kitty passed by and wanted to know,
What are you doing,
my handsome little men?
Making fine coats for gentlemen.
Shall I come in and cut off
your threads?
Oh no, Kitty, you would
bite off our heads!

The singing mice
made Tomkin hungry.
Tomkin wanted mice
and milk for supper.

Tomkin tried to pull the latch on the door, but the key was in the pocket of the tailor's old coat. He settled down on the window ledge and watched as the little mice sewed the mayor's new wedding suit.

Near dawn, Tomkin heard the mice cry, "No more golden thread!"

Tomkin jumped down from the window ledge and went up the steps to the tailor's tiny room. He found the tailor sleeping peacefully without a fever. The cat got the spool of golden thread from the teapot and placed it upon the tailor's quilt. Tomkin curled up beside the tailor.

"Tomkin, clever cat! You did get my thread," said the tailor. He jumped up from bed and hurried into his old coat.

"It's the mayor's wedding day. What will the mayor do for his suit? There is not enough time."

Tomkin led the tailor down to his shop. The tailor unlocked the door and threw it open.

The mice had all scattered, but there on the table where the tailor had left the pieces of satin and silk was the loveliest emerald wedding suit he had ever seen.

The suit was stitched with gold.
The vest was trimmed with lace.
Everything was finished —
everything but one buttonhole.

There was a scrap of paper pinned to
the buttonhole, which read "no more
golden thread" in tiny writing.

The tailor finished the buttonhole with the
thread Tomkin had bought. It was perfect.

The mayor was very pleased. People came
from far and wide to buy the tailor's fine
suits. The tailor became very rich. And his
cat, Tomkin, grew very fat!

Little Red Riding Hood

Adapted by Julie Reich

Illustrated by Thea Kliros

Once upon a time, a girl lived with her mother in a small village on the edge of a forest. All of the villagers loved the girl. They called her Little Red Riding Hood because she wore a red hooded cape that her grandmother made for her.

Little Red Riding Hood's grandmother lived alone in the middle of the forest. One day, Little Red Riding Hood's mother said, "Grandmother is sick. Please take her this basket of cookies, breads, and muffins. She is expecting you, so go straight to her house. Do not stray from the path."

"All right, Mother," said Little Red Riding Hood, and she set off with the basket.

Little Red Riding Hood was happy.
She liked to go to Grandmother's house.

She liked the forest, too. She looked at the
tall trees. She sniffed the pretty flowers.
She listened to the singing birds.

A wicked wolf was watching Little Red
Riding Hood. She did not see him.
He was hiding behind a tree.

The wolf was happy to see her!
He liked to eat little girls.

The wolf smiled and said, "Mmmm.
I will eat her for lunch."

The wolf did not dare to eat the girl while they were in the forest, because he knew that the woodcutter might come by. Just that morning, the wolf had seen the woodcutter use his sharp ax to chop down a tree.

When Little Red Riding Hood passed by his tree, the wolf stepped out and said, "Hello, little girl. What is your name?"

Little Red Riding Hood was friendly to everybody, and she did not know that wolves like to eat people. "My name is Little Red Riding Hood," she said.

"What are you doing out so early?" asked the wolf.

"I am going to visit my grandmother," said Little Red Riding Hood.

"What do you have in your basket?" asked the wolf.

"I have cookies, breads, and muffins for my grandmother," said Little Red Riding Hood. "She is sick."

"Where does your grandmother live?" asked the wolf.

"She lives in the middle of the forest," said Little Red Riding Hood. "Her house has a pretty white fence and a bright red door."

The wolf had an idea. He picked some white flowers.
"Take these flowers to your grandmother," said the wolf.

"Thank you," said Little Red Riding Hood.

"But wait," said the wolf, "those are all white. I see yellow flowers, too."

"And I see pink flowers," said Little Red Riding Hood.

Little Red Riding Hood walked away from the path. She picked the yellow and pink flowers.

She did not see the wolf run away.

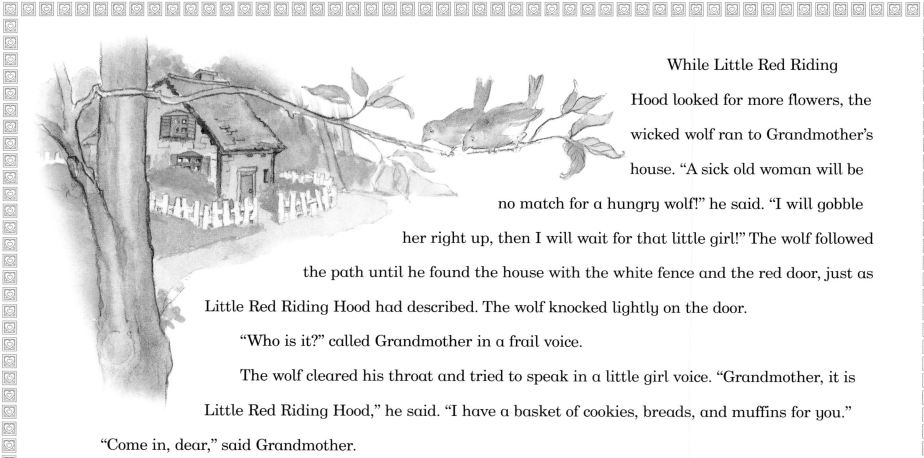

While Little Red Riding Hood looked for more flowers, the wicked wolf ran to Grandmother's house. "A sick old woman will be no match for a hungry wolf!" he said. "I will gobble her right up, then I will wait for that little girl!" The wolf followed the path until he found the house with the white fence and the red door, just as Little Red Riding Hood had described. The wolf knocked lightly on the door.

"Who is it?" called Grandmother in a frail voice.

The wolf cleared his throat and tried to speak in a little girl voice. "Grandmother, it is Little Red Riding Hood," he said. "I have a basket of cookies, breads, and muffins for you."

"Come in, dear," said Grandmother.

The wolf was surprised to find Grandmother folding and arranging blankets in the closet, instead of lying in bed. Grandmother was just as surprised to see a wolf in her doorway! She screamed, pulled the closet door shut, and locked herself in.

The wolf tried to open the closet door. He pushed. He pulled. He banged. He bumped. The door did not budge.

"Oh, well," said the wolf. "I will just wait for Little Red Riding Hood. She is the one I want to eat."

The wolf dressed like Grandmother. He put on her cap. He put on her gown. Then he climbed into the bed and pulled the quilt up to his long nose. The wolf waited and waited and waited for the little girl and her basket of goodies.

Finally, Little Red Riding Hood knocked on the door and went inside.

"You do not look well, Grandmother," said Little Red Riding Hood leaning in for a closer look.

"No, I do not feel well," said the wolf. "Come closer, my dear."

"Grandmother, what big eyes you have!" cried Little Red Riding Hood.

"The better to see you with, my dear," said the wolf trying to sound like Grandmother.

"And what big ears you have!" said Little Red Riding Hood.

"The better to hear you with, my dear," said the wolf.

"And what big hands you have!" said Little Red Riding Hood

"The better to hug you with, my dear," said the wolf.

"And what big teeth you have!" cried Little Red Riding Hood.

"The better to EAT you with!" the wolf shouted as he threw back the quilt and jumped out of bed.

Little Red Riding Hood screamed. She ran. The wolf ran after her. "I will get you!" the wolf yelled.

Little Red Riding Hood screamed again. She ran to the back of the house. She ran to the front of the house. She kept running. The wolf kept running after her.

"I will get you!" the wolf yelled.

Then Little Red Riding Hood had an idea. She threw a chair onto the floor. The wolf fell over it. Little Red Riding Hood ran outside.

The wicked wolf ran after her.

The wolf caught up to Little Red Riding Hood. He reached to grab Little Red Riding Hood's cape when he saw the woodcutter holding his ax in the air.

"Stop!" the woodcutter shouted to the wolf.

The wolf disappeared into the forest.

Little Red Riding Hood began to cry.

"Don't cry," said the woodcutter. "You are safe."

"But what about Grandmother?" she cried.

"The wolf must have eaten her! Mother told me not to stop on the way and not to stray from the path. I only wanted to bring Grandmother something beautiful to make her feel better."

Suddenly they heard a soft voice. "Little Red Riding Hood?" Grandmother was standing in the doorway!

"You are alive!" cried Little Red Riding Hood.

"I am all right. I was in the closet," said Grandmother.

"Thank you for saving us," Little Red Riding Hood said to the woodcutter.

"Yes, that was very kind of you," agreed Grandmother.

"Little Red Riding Hood is always kind to the whole village," said the woodcutter. "I am glad I could help."

"I am glad that we are all safe," Grandmother said.

"And I am glad I have learned my lesson," Little Red Riding Hood said. "I will always listen to Mother. And I will never talk to a wolf again!"

The End